Little Book
of
Nursery
Tales

Retold by
Verónica Uribe

Translated by
Susan Ouriou

Illustrated by
Carmen Salvador

Groundwood Books

House of Anansi Press

Table of Contents

 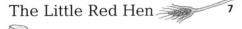

A little red hen was pecking the ground in the barnyard when she found a small grain of wheat. "Look what I found!" she exclaimed.

The duck, the cow and the cat all came over to have a look at the seed of wheat.

"Who will help me sow the seed?" the little red hen asked.

"Not I," said the duck.

"Not I," said the cow.

"Not I," said the cat.

"Well then, if no one wants to help me, I'll sow the seed by myself," said the little red hen. And she set off by herself to sow her grain of wheat.

When the wheat had grown and ripened, the little red hen asked, "Who will help me harvest the wheat?"

"Not I," said the duck.

"Not I," said the cow.

"Not I," said the cat.

"Well then, if no one wants to help me, I'll harvest it by myself," said the little red hen. And she set off by herself to harvest the wheat.

Once the wheat was harvested, the

little red hen asked, "Who will help me take the wheat to the mill to have it ground into flour?"

"Not I," said the duck.

"Not I," said the cow.

"Not I," said the cat.

"Well then, if no one wants to help me, I'll take it to the flour mill by myself," said the little red hen. And she set off by herself to have the wheat ground.

When the wheat was ground into flour, the little red hen asked, "Who will help me make the bread?"

"Not I," said the duck.

"Not I," said the cow.

"Not I," said the cat.

"Well then, if no one wants to help me, I'll make the bread by myself," said the little red hen. And she set off by herself to make the bread.

Once the loaf of bread came out of the oven, golden and sweet-smelling, the little red hen asked, "Who will help me eat the bread?"

"I will!" quacked the duck.

"I will!" mooed the cow.

"I will!" meowed the cat.

"Oh, no, you won't!" said the little red hen. "I'm going to eat it all by myself!"

Goldlilocks and the Three Bears

Once upon a time, three bears lived together in a little house in the middle of the forest. Papa Bear was a great big bear. Mama Bear was a medium-sized bear. Baby Bear was a wee little bear.

One day, Mama Bear prepared a breakfast of porridge and honey. She poured the porridge into three bowls. While they waited for their porridge to

cool, the three bears went for a walk through the forest.

Soon after, a little girl named Goldilocks arrived. She drew near to the bears' house and since the door was ajar, she peered in. She looked to the left, then to the right and, seeing no one, she decided to go inside.

She saw the table set with three bowls of porridge and realized how hungry she was.

First, she tried the porridge in the great big bowl, but it was too hot.

Next, she tried the porridge in the medium-sized bowl, but it was too thick.

Then she tried the porridge in the wee little bowl, and it was so delicious she ate it all up.

When she had finished, Goldilocks decided to sit down for a bit of a rest.

First, she sat in the great big chair, but it was too high.

Next, she sat in the medium-sized chair, but it was too wide.

Then she sat in the wee little chair, and it felt just right. But the chair was too little for Goldilocks, and it broke.

Afterwards, Goldilocks felt sleepy and decided to lie down for a nap. She went upstairs where she found three beds.

First, she lay down on the great big bed, but it was too hard.

Next, she lay down on the medium-sized bed, but it was too soft.

Finally she lay down on the wee little bed, and it was so cozy she fell fast asleep.

As she slept, the three bears returned from their walk.

Papa Bear saw a spoon in his bowl and roared in a thundering voice, "Someone has been eating my porridge!"

Mama Bear saw a spoon in her bowl and squealed in a high, piercing voice, "Someone has been eating my porridge!"

Baby Bear looked at his bowl and

cried in a wee little voice, "Someone has been eating my porridge and they've eaten it all up!"

Papa Bear walked over to his chair, saw the cushion out of place and roared in a thundering voice, "Someone has been sitting in my chair!"

Mama Bear went over to her chair, saw the cushion out of place and squealed in a high, piercing voice, "Someone has been sitting in my chair!"

Baby Bear looked at his chair and cried in a wee little voice, "Someone has been sitting in my chair and they've broken it!"

The three bears made their way upstairs.

Papa Bear saw his rumpled bed and roared in a thundering voice, "Someone has been sleeping in my bed!"

Mama Bear saw her rumpled bed and squealed in a high, piercing voice, "Someone has been sleeping in my bed!"

Baby Bear looked at his bed and cried in a wee little voice, "Someone has been sleeping in my bed and she's still here!"

On hearing their cries, Goldilocks woke up in a fright. She jumped out of bed, flew down the stairs and ran and ran. She didn't stop running until she had left the forest far behind.

And she never went back to the three bears' house again.

The Seven Little Kids

There were once seven little kids who lived with their mother goat in a house in the woods.

But a mean old wolf lived in the woods, too.

One day, their mother had to go to the market. She called together her seven little kids and said, "Make sure you lock the door, and don't open it to anyone in case it's the mean old wolf."

"How will we know if the mean old wolf comes knocking at our door?" asked one of the little kids.

"By his rough voice and his black feet," their mother said, then bade them goodbye.

As soon as she left, the seven little kids locked and bolted the door.

The wolf, who had been hiding behind some bushes, saw the mother goat making her way to town and thought, "At last I can treat myself to the seven oh so plump and tender kids."

He reached their door in three bounds. *Knock, knock, knock!*

"Who is it?"

"Open up, little kids. It's your mother, home from the market. I've brought you some candy," said the wolf.

But the little kids answered, "Oh, no, you're not our mother. Her voice is sweet and yours is rough."

So the wolf returned home and ate six spoonfuls of honey to sweeten his voice.

He went back to the little kids' house. *Knock, knock, knock!*

"Who is it?"

"Open up, little kids. It's your mother, home from the market. I've brought you some candy," the wolf said in a sweet voice.

The little kids started to open the door, but as soon as they caught sight of the wolf's feet they slammed it shut and said, "Oh, no, you're not our mother. Her feet are white and yours are black."

The wolf was furious. He stormed over to the miller's house and told him to throw flour on his feet. The miller blanketed the wolf's feet in white flour.

The wolf raced back to the little kids' house. *Knock, knock, knock!*

"Who is it?"

"Open up, little kids. It's your mother, home from the market. I've brought you some candy," the wolf said.

"First, show us your feet," the little kids answered, peering underneath the door.

The wolf showed them his flour-covered feet. Then the little kids opened the door.

The wolf leapt into the house and all the little kids raced for cover.

The first little kid hid in the laundry basket. The second little kid hid under the bed. The third little kid hid in a desk drawer. The fourth little kid hid under the table. The fifth little kid hid in the cupboard. The sixth little kid hid behind the couch. And the littlest kid hid inside the clock.

But the mean old wolf found them one by one, and one by one he gobbled them down. All except the littlest kid, because the wolf never thought to look inside the clock.

The wolf left with a full belly and lay down for a nap under a tree in the middle of the woods.

When their mother came back from the market, she found the door open and her house a shambles. "Oh, me, my children. Oh, my, my little kids! The wolf has eaten you all."

"Not me! Not me!" cried the littlest kid from inside the clock.

His mother helped him out and the

little kid told her what had happened. When he finished, the mother goat fetched her scissors, a spool of thread, a needle and a thimble, took her only little kid by the hand, and went into the woods in search of the wolf.

They walked and they walked until they heard snoring. The wolf lay fast asleep under a tree.

The mother goat tiptoed up and slashed open the wolf's belly with her scissors. All the little kids jumped out, one after the other. The wolf slept so soundly he did not notice a thing. The little kids skipped for joy, but the mother goat told them, "Shhh . . . don't wake

up the wolf. We're not finished yet. Find me six big rocks to put inside the wolf's belly."

The little kids did as they were told. Then the mother goat threaded the needle and carefully sewed up the wolf's belly.

The mother goat and the little kids made their way back home. Once barricaded inside, they ate all the candy she had brought home from the market.

In the meantime, the wolf woke up with a bellyache. He tried to walk to the river to get some water, but he could barely budge because his belly weighed so much.

"Ouch! Those little kids are not as tender as I thought," he lamented.

When he stooped over to drink from the river, the weight of the stones in his belly dragged him off the riverbank and—*splash!*—into the water.

The wolf was swept away by the current, never to be seen again by the mother goat and her seven little kids.

The Three Little Pigs

There were once three little pigs who decided to set out on their own to seek their fortune.

The first little pig met up with a farmer carrying a bundle of straw.

"Mr. Farmer," said the little pig, "would you give me some straw so I can build a house?"

"With pleasure," the farmer said, and he gave the little pig some straw.

The little pig began building his

house — *swish, swoosh, swish* — and as he worked, he sang a little song:

Here I'll live in a house of straw so fine

I've built a home that I can call all mine

And never will I let the big, bad wolf inside

The next day his house was ready. The little pig was very pleased with how fine his house looked. He stepped inside and shut the door behind him.

The second little pig met up with a woodsman carrying an armload of sticks.

"Mr. Woodsman," said the little pig, "would you give me a few sticks so I can build a house?"

"With pleasure," said the woodsman,

and he gave the little pig a few sticks.

The little pig began building his house — *tap, tappity, tap* — and as he worked, he sang a little song:

Here I'll live in a house of sticks so fine

I've built a home that I can call all mine

And never will I let the big, bad wolf inside

It took him four days to finish his house. When it was ready, the little pig was very pleased with how fine his house looked. He stepped inside and closed the door behind him.

The third little pig met up with a bricklayer pushing a wheelbarrow full of bricks.

"Mr. Bricklayer," said the little pig,

"would you give me some bricks so I can build a house?"

"With pleasure," said the bricklayer, and he gave the little pig some bricks.

The little pig began building his house — *scritch, scratch, scritch, scratch* — and while he worked, he sang a little song:

Here I'll live in a house of bricks so fine

I've built a home that I can call all mine

And never will I let the big, bad wolf inside

It took him over a week to finish. When his house was ready, the little pig was very pleased at how nice and solid it looked. He stepped inside with a great deal of satisfaction and closed the door behind him.

Soon afterwards, the wolf arrived at the first little pig's straw house and said, "Little pig, little pig, let me come in."

"Not by the hair of my chinny-chin-chin," the little pig said.

"You'll be sorry! I'll huff and I'll puff and I'll blow your straw house in."

The wolf took a big breath, then he huffed and he puffed and he blew the straw house in.

The wolf leapt inside, but the little pig ran to his brother's house to hide.

The wolf arrived at the second little pig's stick house and said, "Little pig, little pig, let me come in."

"Not by the hair of my chinny-chin-

chin," said the second little pig.

"You'll be sorry! I'll huff and I'll puff and I'll blow your stick house in."

The wolf took a big breath, then he huffed and he puffed and he blew the stick house in.

The wolf leapt inside, but the two little pigs ran to their brother's house to hide.

The wolf arrived at the third little pig's brick house and called out once more, "Little pig, little pig, let me come in."

"Not by the hair of my chinny-chin-chin."

"You'll be sorry! I'll huff and I'll puff and I'll blow your house in."

The wolf took a great big gulp of air. He huffed and he puffed and he huffed and he puffed and... the brick house didn't budge.

The wolf was getting very angry. He huffed and he puffed as hard as he could, with every last breath of air in his lungs... but the third little pig's brick house didn't budge.

Then the wolf took a great big huge gulp of air and he huffed and he puffed and he huffed and he puffed again and again and... the little brick house didn't budge.

Furious, the wolf climbed a nearby tree and jumped onto the roof of the

brick house. He began to climb down the chimney. But the three little pigs had put a big pot of water over the fire. The wolf slid down the chimney, straight into the pot of boiling water. By the time he escaped, there was not a single hair left on his body.

The three little pigs never saw the wolf again.

Half-a-Chick

Once upon a time, a hen settled into her nest to lay her eggs. Twenty-one days later, the baby chicks began to hatch. Nine cute little chicks broke through their shells. But the last chick to hatch was very strange-looking indeed. He had only one eye, one wing and one leg.

Seeing him, his mother named him Half-a-Chick.

Half-a-Chick skipped around the barnyard behind his brothers, hippity-hopping on his one leg and doing whatever he felt like. When his mother called the little chicks back to the nest—*cluck, cluck, cluck*—Half-a-Chick ran the other way. When their mother taught them to scratch and peck at the ground for food, Half-a-Chick lay down for a nap.

One day, Half-a-Chick said to his mother, "I'm tired of the barnyard. I'm going to the palace to see the king."

"The palace is a long way away," his mother said. "And you're too little to make such a long trip alone. Don't go yet. Some day I'll take you there."

But Half-a-Chick did not want to wait, so he shook his half-a-head and said, "I'm going right away."

And he did. He skipped away from the barnyard on his one leg, hippity-hop, hippity-hop.

Soon Half-a-Chick came across a stream choked with weeds.

The stream said, "Half-a-Chick, help me. Pull out these weeds with your half-a-beak. They're strangling me and won't let my water flow."

But Half-a-Chick answered,

I'm off to the palace to see the king;

I have no time for dawdling.

Hippity-hop, hippity-hop, he hurried on his way.

Soon after, Half-a-Chick came across a fire about to die out.

The fire said, "Half-a-Chick, help me. Find some dry branches with your half-a-beak and bring them to me so I won't die."

But Half-a-Chick answered,

I'm going to the palace to see the king;

I have no time for dawdling.

Hippity-hop, hippity-hop, he hurried on his way.

Farther on, Half-a-Chick came across the wind caught in some bushes.

The wind said, "Half-a-Chick, help me. Push aside these bushes with your half-a-beak so I can keep on blowing."

But Half-a-Chick answered,

I'm off to the palace to see the king;

I have no time for dawdling.

Hippity-hop, hippity-hop, he hurried on his way.

Finally, Half-a-Chick reached the palace. "Now I'll be able to see the king," he thought happily.

But just then the palace cook caught

sight of him, grabbed him by the neck and carried him into the kitchen.

"Just what I needed. The king feels like chicken soup for supper," the cook said as he dropped Half-a-Chick into a pot of water.

"Water! Water! Help me! I'm drowning," cried Half-a-Chick.

But the water answered, "I was the stream being choked by weeds, but you didn't want to help me then. So I won't help you now."

The cook lit the fire.

"Fire! Fire! Help me! I'm burning," cried Half-a-Chick.

But the fire answered, "I was dying and you didn't want to help me. So I won't help you now."

Half-a-Chick had already begun to burn when the wind blew past. It plunged into the pot like a whirlwind, lifted Half-a-Chick up high in the air and carried him out of the kitchen.

"Thank you, wind. You may put me down now," said Half-a-Chick.

But the wind answered, "I was caught in the bushes, but you didn't want to help me. So I won't help you now."

The wind blew even harder and lifted

Half-a-Chick to the very top of the bell tower and left him there.

Today, the weathercock can still be seen high up on the bell tower with his one leg and his one wing, watching with his one eye to see which way the wind is blowing.

Cucaracha Martínez

As she swept the sidewalk in front of her house one day, Cucaracha Martínez came upon a silver coin. Happily, she thought, "What shall I buy myself with this coin? What shall it be? Toffee? Caramels? Candy? No, no sweets. I'll buy myself a bright guava-colored dress instead."

Her mind made up, Cucaracha Martínez dropped the coin into her pocket and continued to sweep. As she swept, she came upon another coin. Would wonders never cease!

"What shall I buy with this coin? What shall it be? Chocolates? Pineapple pull? Fig bars? No, no sweets. I'll buy myself a purple ribbon instead."

Her mind made up, Cucaracha Martínez picked up the coin, then kept on sweeping the sidewalk.

As she swept, she came upon another coin. How wonderful!

"What shall I buy myself with this coin? Dearie me, what shall I buy?

Coconut treats? Mango jelly? Honey peanuts? No, no sweets. I'll buy myself a box of scented powder instead."

Her mind made up, Cucaracha Martínez set off for the store to buy herself a dress, a ribbon and a box of scented powder. Back home, she had a bath, dusted herself with powder, put on her new dress and tied the ribbon in her hair. Then she sat ever so prettily on her front doorstep.

The bull passed by and said, "Cucaracha Martínez, how pretty you look today!"

"If you say so, then it must be true," she said sweetly.

The admiring bull asked, "Cucaracha, will you marry me?"

"What will you say before we go to sleep at night?" she asked.

"*Mooo! Mooo!*" the bull bellowed with all his might.

"Dear me, no! You'll frighten me!" said Cucaracha Martínez. "No, bull, I won't marry you."

The bull left, sad and broken-hearted.

Next the dog passed by and said,

"Cucaracha Martínez, how pretty you look today!"

"If you say so, it must be true," she answered sweetly.

The admiring dog asked, "Cucaracha, will you marry me?"

"What will you say to me before we go to sleep at night?" she asked.

"*Woof! Woof!*" barked the dog with all his might.

"Dear me, no! You'll frighten me!" she replied. "No, dog, I won't marry you."

The sad dog left, his tail between his legs.

The rooster passed by and said, "Cucaracha Martínez, how pretty you look today!"

"If you say so, it must be true," she said sweetly.

The admiring rooster asked, "Cucaracha, will you marry me?"

"What will you say before we go to sleep at night?" she asked.

"*Cock-a-doodle-doo! Cock-a-doodle-doo!*" crowed the rooster with all his might.

"Dear me, no! You'll frighten me!" she replied. "No, rooster, I won't marry you."

The sad rooster left, his cock's comb drooping.

It was getting dark by the time Ratón Pérez walked by.

"Cucaracha Martínez, how beautiful you look today!"

"If you say so, it must be true," she answered sweetly.

A lovestruck Ratón Pérez said, "Cucaracha, will you marry me?"

"What will you say before we go to sleep at night?" she asked.

"*Chiree . . . Chiree . . . Chiree . . .* and I'll love you just like this," Ratón Pérez said softly as he kissed Cucaracha.

This she liked very much, and she married Ratón Pérez.

The day after the wedding, Cucaracha Martínez went off to the market and asked Ratón Pérez to watch the pot on the stove.

"Remember to stir it now and then, but use the big spoon," she warned before leaving.

Ratón Pérez loved food and wanted to see what smelled so good. He forgot Cucaracha Martínez's warning, however, and instead of a big spoon, he took a wee little spoon and climbed up the side of the pot. Oh, what a delicious-looking

stew, with a golden onion floating right on top!

Ratón Pérez tried to reach the onion with the little spoon, but it was too far away. He stretched as far as he could, then a little farther still, until he began to totter back and forth, only to fall—*splash!*—into the pot. Poor Ratón Pérez! He drowned on the spot.

When Cucaracha Martínez returned from the market, she looked high and low for Ratón Pérez. She looked in the living room, she looked in the bedroom, she looked in the bathroom, but he wasn't to be found anywhere. Finally, she went into the kitchen to stir the stew and she realized what had happened.

Cucaracha Martínez started to cry and ran out of her house singing,

Drawn by the flavor

And wishing to savor

Ratón fell into the stew

What is Cucaracha to do?

How Ratón Pérez Came Back to Life

Cucaracha Martínez would not be comforted as she sat weeping on her front doorstep over the loss of Ratón Pérez.

A little bird passed by and asked, "Cucaracha, why are you crying?"

She sighed sadly and said,

> **Because drawn by the flavor**
>
> **And wishing to savor**
>
> **Ratón fell into the stew.**

What is Cucaracha to do?

Hearing her, the little bird chopped off his beak.

As he flew and flew, the little bird met up with a dove who asked him, "Little bird, why did you chop off your beak?"

The sad little bird answered,

Drawn by the flavor

And wishing to savor

Ratón fell into the stew.

What is Cucaracha to do?

Hearing him, the dove cut off her tail feathers.

The dove went to fetch some water from the spring, and the spring asked,

"Dove, why did you cut off your plumage?"

The sad dove answered,

> Because in his grief
> Bird chopped off his beak
> Because drawn by the flavor
> And wishing to savor
> Ratón fell into the stew.
> What is Cucaracha to do?

Hearing her, the spring stopped her water from flowing.

Ramón came to the spring for water and seeing her water all dried up, he asked, "Spring, why did you stop your water from flowing?"

The sad spring answered,

> **Because in her anguish**
>
> **Dove cut off her plumage**
>
> **Because in his grief**
>
> **Bird chopped off his beak**
>
> **Because drawn by the flavor**
>
> **And wishing to savor**
>
> **Ratón fell into the stew.**
>
> **What is Cucaracha to do?**

Hearing her, Ramón dropped and broke his jug.

On his return, the lady of the house asked, "Ramón, why did you break your jug?"

A sad Ramón answered,

Because in her woe

The spring stopped her flow

Because in her anguish

Dove cut off her plumage

Because in his grief

Bird chopped off his beak

Because drawn by the flavor

And wishing to savor

Ratón fell into the stew.

What is Cucaracha to do?

Hearing him, the lady of the house said, "We'll fix this right away."

She and Ramón ran to find the doctor. The dove and the little bird flew behind.

The doctor grabbed his bag, and

together they ran to Cucaracha's house. They managed to fish Ratón Pérez out of the stew, wash him off, lay him down on his bed and give him a massage with coconut oil. The doctor took his pulse and put a few bitter drops in his mouth. Ratón Pérez sneezed and opened his eyes.

As soon as Cucaracha Martínez saw that Ratón Pérez had been saved, she rushed to the kitchen to make a paste of flour and water for glue. The bird got his beak and ended his grief. The dove got her plumage and so cured her anguish. Ramón got his jug, and gave thanks with a hug.

What about the doctor? He prescribed some camphor.

What about the lady? She picked herself a daisy.

What about the spring? She flowed gaily and began to sing:

> Our tale began on a front sidewalk,
>
> Followed a mouse down into a pot,
>
> And ended when all had found
>
> what they sought.

Nursery Rhymes

A Mouse's Tail

A very old mouse, quite stooped and frail,
Did somehow manage to iron her tail.
She did not see beneath her dress,
The part of herself she managed to press.

At that spot was left a stub,
On which some cream she smoothed
and rubbed.
A hankie she found inside a big bag,
And made of her tail a bright
cheery flag.

The Motley Mob

Twenty mice, some skinny, some stout,
Scurried through alleys, up, down, round
about.
Out in front a she mouse held the lead,
Close behind ran her mob at top speed.

Some had teeth both long and
pointy,
Others had teeth quite short and fine;
Some had eyes both small and
beady,
Others had eyes quite
big and wide.

Some had feet both thin and
    scrabbly,
Others had feet quite big and
    broad;
Some had tails both slim and
    wispy,
Others had tails quite thick and stout.

Some had ears both large and floppy,
Others had ears quite sharp and spry;
Some had snouts both long and droopy,
Others had snouts that twitched alive.

María, María

"María, María
Come and sweep!"
   "I have no hands
I have no feet."

"María, María
Come and sew!"
   "I have no hands
Nor feet or toes."

"María, María
Come and grind!"
   "I have no hands
Nor feet, I find."

"María, María
Come and eat!"
   "I've found my hands
And look! Two feet!"

Pimpimarantula

Pimpimarantula
Here comes the tarantula,
Asking for a book of psalms
For prayers to keep him calm.

Pimpimaringale
Here comes the nightingale,
Asking for some millet
To throw into her skillet.

Pimpimarurell
Here comes the squirrel,
Asking for a bowtie
Of silk to dazzle passersby.

Pimpimarallion
Here comes the stallion,
Asking for a bit of cash
So he can have a bigger stash.

Pimpimaranzee
Here comes the chimpanzee,
Asking for some fruit to eat
Beneath his favorite tree.

AEIOU

Anxious Antonine,
The flitting honeybee,
Cries, "I feel so lonely,
A mate is what I need.
I know the one for me, he's . . ."

Edmund oh so elegant,
Who's, by the way, an elephant,
Says, "Not to seem too arrogant,
A bee is not for me.
There's someone else you see,
she's . . ."

Izzie, the iguana,
Lolls idly in the sauna,
"Edmund's not the fauna
With whom I'd like to be.
I know who's right for me, he's . . ."

Oliver, the old-time bear,
Who's very, very well aware,
"That Izzie, see, she has no hair,
And is too slim for me.
I know who she should be, it's . . .

Unsung magpie Ursuline,
Who says, "For Anxious Antonine,
Idly lolling Izzie,
Edmund oh so elegant,
And Oliver the bear,
Some cakes I'll bake to share."

A E I O U
Which one is right for you?

About the Nursery Tales

There are tales that travel the world with ease and grace. Over the years, they become part of the written and oral traditions of the people who encounter them. These brief stories originated in Europe before traveling across the ocean to the Americas.

In *Little Book of Nursery Tales*, you will find seven of the most popular nursery stories, all of which maintain the essence of the European tradition while assimilating a certain Creole flavor. These tales were selected for small children whose parents and grandparents will be reading to them, since almost nothing is quite as delightful as listening to a good story told with love.

Each of the nursery tales in this collection has its own history.

Goldilocks was originally an old Scottish tale about a fox that enters the bears' home without permission. Over time, the fox evolved into an old woman and, later yet, into a girl with golden locks. An episode similar to the scene in which Goldilocks tries the porridge, the chairs and the beds appears in *Snow White*.

The Seven Little Kids can be found in the stories by the Brothers Grimm under the title *The Wolf and the Seven Little Kids*. The story remains virtually unchanged, including the details of the wolf's feet being blanketed in flour and the littlest goat hiding inside the clock to escape from the wolf.

The Three Little Pigs comes from a story published in England in 1813. By building a solid brick house, the oldest of three geese tricks the fox that wants to eat them.

Half-a-Chick is a Spanish tale, well known in the Basque country. In the original version, Half-a-Chick finds a money pouch as he is scratching for food in the chicken coop. The king's son passes by and asks to borrow the pouch, which he never gives back. This version differs in many respects from the original, but is the one best known in the Americas.

Cucaracha Martínez appears in A.R. Almodóvar's collection of Spanish tales. The anecdote is similar, but the protagonist, originally a coquettish ant, evolved into a cockroach—a *cucaracha*—in several Latin American countries. Ratón Pérez is actually an insect found in Andalusia called *ratompérez*. Over time, it became known as the mouse Ratón Pérez.

How Ratón Pérez Came Back to Life is a sequel to the above-mentioned tale that softens its sad ending. It is constructed as a cumulative tale and is told in many countries of the Caribbean.

We have no source for **The Little Red Hen**, but its repetitive structure and moralizing intent suggest that it originated as a fable.

V.U.

Bibliography

Almodóvar, A.R. *Cuentos al amor de la lumbre*.
Madrid: Ediciones Generales Anaya, 1984.

Bettelheim, Bruno, *Psicoanálisis de los cuentos de hadas*. Barcelona: Editorial Crítica, 1978.

Carpenter, Humphrey and Mari Prichard. *The Oxford Companion to Children's Literature*. Oxford: Oxford University Press, 1987.

Grimm, J. and W. *Cuentos de niños y del hogar*.
Madrid: Ediciones Generales Anaya, 1985.

Opie, Iona and Peter. *The Classic Fairy Tales*. New York: Oxford University Press, 1980.

First published in Spanish as El libro de oro de los niños
copyright © 1996 Ediciones Ekaré, Caracas, Venezuela
First published in English by Groundwood Books
English translation copyright © 2005 by Susan Ouriou

Groundwood Books / House of Anansi Press
110 Spadina Avenue, Suite 801, Toronto, Ontario M5V 2K4
Distributed in the USA by Publishers Group West
1700 Fourth Street, Berkeley, CA 94710

Library and Archives Canada Cataloging in Publication
Uribe, Verónica
Little book of nursery tales / retold by Verónica Uribe ; translated by
Susan Ouriou ; illustrated by Carmen Salvador.
Translation of: El libro de oro de los niños.
ISBN 0-88899-673-X
1. Children's stories, Latin American. I. Ouriou, Susan II. Salvador, Carmen III. Title
PZ8.U74Lin 2005   j863   C2005-902255-8

Art direction by Irene Savino
Printed and bound in China